Level 1 is ideal for children who have received some initial reading instruction. Each story is told very simply, using a small number of frequently repeated words.

Special features:

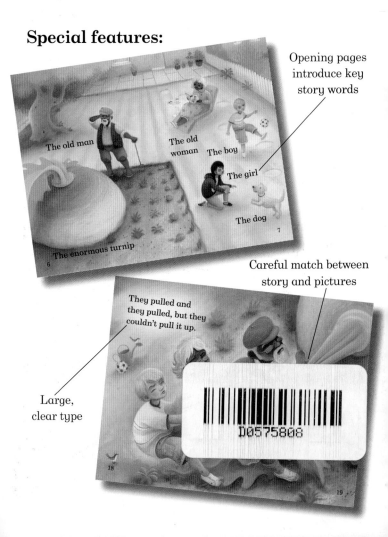

Opening pages introduce key story words

The old man

The old woman

The boy

The girl

The dog

The enormous turnip

Careful match between story and pictures

They pulled and they pulled, but they couldn't pull it up.

Large, clear type

D0575808

Educational Consultant: Geraldine Taylor
Book Banding Consultant: Kate Ruttle

A catalogue record for this book is available from the British Library

Published by Ladybird Books Ltd
80 Strand, London, WC2R 0RL
A Penguin Company

002
© LADYBIRD BOOKS LTD MMX. This edition MMXIII
Ladybird, Read It Yourself and the Ladybird Logo are registered or
unregistered trademarks of Ladybird Books Limited.

ISBN: 978-0-72327-279-3

Printed in China

The Enormous Turnip

Illustrated by Richard Johnson

The old man

The enormous turnip

The old woman

The boy

The girl

The dog

The old man planted some turnip seeds.

The turnip seeds grew and grew.

One turnip grew enormous.

"I want that enormous turnip for my tea," said the old man.

He pulled and he pulled, but he couldn't pull it up.

11

The old man called
to the old woman.

"Help me pull up this
enormous turnip,"
he said.

They pulled and
they pulled, but they
couldn't pull it up.

15

The old woman
called to the boy.

"Help us pull up this
enormous turnip,"
she said.

17

They pulled and
they pulled, but they
couldn't pull it up.

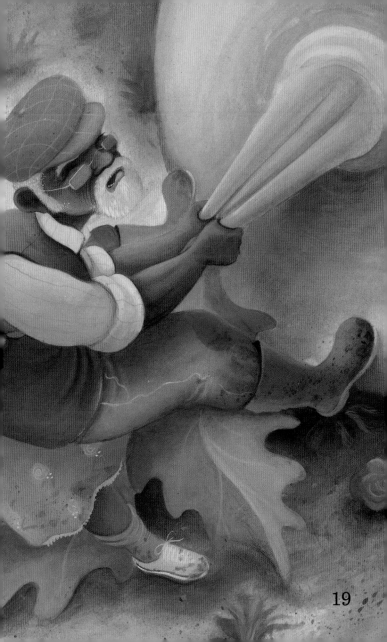

19

The boy called
to the girl.

"Help us pull up
this enormous
turnip," he said.

They pulled and
they pulled, but they
couldn't pull it up.

23

The girl called to the dog.

"Help us pull up this
enormous turnip,"
she said.

They pulled and
they pulled and
they pulled.

Up popped the
enormous turnip!

And they all had
turnip for tea.

28

How much do you remember about the story of The Enormous Turnip? Answer these questions and find out!

- What does the old man plant?

- Who does the old man ask to help him pull up the enormous turnip?

- Who does the girl ask to help her pull up the enormous turnip?